My Frumpy

Reading Sweater

P. Kevin Remington

AEGA Design Publishing Ltd
London, UK

ISBN 978-1-7395166-3-5 (hbk)
ISBN 978-1-7395166-4-2 (pbk)
ISBN 978-1-7395166-5-9 (digital)

To Kyle and Stephanie,
my fellow campers

Contents

Preface

In March of 2020, due to COVID-19, I decided that everyone needed a break and distraction from the overwhelming pandemic. The question was, what exactly could I do to help? I could not sing well enough to make a video recording for all to enjoy. I am more a shower singer. I also wanted this to be a recurring event. Having a single video would not have achieved my purpose.

I have been told that I can tell a story well. My daughter sug-gested that I read children's stories and post them online. That was just the solution and venue for which I was looking.

From March 21 to October 5, I read and told a children's story each day. I cannot say that I had a large following of viewers. I did have regular viewers who really did enjoy my storytelling.

In the 199 stories presented, I included many well-known children's authors and a few lesser known. I also included seventeen that were created by me. I could not say "written by me" until today. I just put on my frumpy reading sweater, sipped my drink of the day, and told the story. This book is a collection of the stories I created.

Humility is not one of my greater virtues, but I must say that I rather enjoyed telling the story and then listening to the story. It was only later after listening to the story that I wrote it down for this book. Now the stories are available for your reading pleasure.

So put on your own frumpy reading sweater and enjoy! If you want to hear me read, or tell, the story, you can find all the stories on YouTube. Search for "Kev Rem Story Time."

P. Kevin Remington
December 24, 2020

The One-Stone Castle

P. Kevin Remington
July 2000

If you travel down this road, down passed the fork in the road and over the hill, you will come to a small kingdom. The people of this small kingdom are a happy people. They all have enough to eat. They all have homes with beds. The children are happy and play in the streets. The streets are safe.

If you were to ask any of the people of this kingdom why they are so safe and happy, they would all say, "It is because of our good king."

If you follow the road through the village and up the hill, you will find at the end of the road a man sitting on a great stone. This man is the king.

The king sits on a large stone that was cut from the Sunshine Mountains on the far edge of the kingdom. He is a great man with a kingdom and people who love him. He is like every other king. He collects taxes. He takes care of the roads and byways to keep them safe. He ensures that each of his subjects has enough to eat. The only difference of this king from other kings is that he has no castle.

If you were to ask this king why he has no castle, he would reply, "I have a magnificent castle. Do you see this great stone that I sit on? It is just a start."

Then the king would give you the tour of his magnificent castle.

"Over here is my entrance if I had one.

"Over here is my throne room where I hold audiences if I had one.

"Over here is my great kitchen where wonderful feasts are prepared if I had one.

"And over here is my bedroom where the king sleeps if I had one."

The king was very proud of telling others about his magnificent castle.

Over the years, other kings would hear of this wonderful king-dom. They would hear how the streets are safe. They would hear about the happy people. And they would hear about how much the people loved the king. All these other kings would hear…and be jealous.

The people in the kingdoms of these other kings did not under-stand. In their kingdoms, the king lived in huge, glorious castles made of stone and glass. Each castle was the envy of other kingdoms, but even with such wonderful castles, their people did not love their kings. Their children did not play happily in the streets. Their streets were not safe. The other kingdoms were very jealous of the happy kingdom.

One day, all the other kingdoms got together and decided to send a delegation to the happy kingdom to see why they were so happy. The delegation was made of kings and princes and lords and ladies from all the other kingdoms.

When the delegation got to the happy kingdom, they first stopped and talked with the children, who happily invited the dele-gation to play hopscotch with them. The delegation said, "No, lords and ladies and kings and princes never play hopscotch!"

Next, the delegation talked with the village mayor who happily invited the delegation to a lunch of soup and cheese and peanut-but-ter sandwiches. The delegation said, "No, lords and ladies and kings and princes never eat such common food!"

The delegation then asked how to find the king of this happy kingdom. They were told to go down the road and up the hill and there they would find the king.

When the delegation went down the road and up the hill, they did not find the king but just a man with an easy smile sitting on a great stone. When they asked to see the king, he told them that he was the king.

The delegation did not believe he was the king for they could not see the king's castle. The king said, "Over here is my entrance if I had one.

"Over here is my throne room where I hold audiences if I had one.

"Over here is my great kitchen where wonderful feasts are prepared if I had one.

"And over here is my bedroom where the king sleeps if I had one."

The king was very proud of telling the delegation about his magnificent castle.

The other kings and princes and lords and ladies were shocked! They were appalled and disgusted because they all had great castles made of stone and glass.

When the king suggested that they might like to play hopscotch with the children or enjoy peanut-butter sandwiches with the mayor, the delegation were completely flabbergasted. With that, the king went off to play with the children and eat lunch with the mayor, and the delegation left the kingdom, never to return.

The next year, when the king had his birthday, all the people planned a special surprise for him.

The mayor invited the king to tour the village with him. All day, they looked at trees and had a lovely time. They watched the children play and had a lovely time. They looked over the farms and fields of grain and had just a lovely day.

While the king was away, the people built a magnificent castle of stone and glass. When the king returned to sit on his great stone, he found, where his great stone sat, a magnificent castle. And when the king looked closer, he found that right there, beside the drawbridge, was the great stone. There was the start of the king's castle.

The people then gave the king a tour of his magnificent castle.

"Over here is your entrance.

"Over here is your throne room where you can hold audiences.

"Over here is your great kitchen where wonderful feasts will be prepared.

"And over here is your bedroom where you will sleep."

The people were very proud of showing the king his magnificent castle.

The king was so overwhelmed with the love of his people that he thanked them all one by one and cried tears of joy.

After living in the magnificent castle, a while, the king was getting restless. He would walk the great halls of his castle and visit his great rooms and look out over the magnificent view. Still the king was getting more and more unhappy.

One night, as the king kissed his son good night, he said, "Son, all this is yours." Then the king tucked in his son as he did every night.

In the morning, when all were awake, they could not find the king.

They looked in the entrance. The king was not there.

They looked in the throne room. The king was not there.

They looked in the kitchen. The king was not there.

They looked in the bedroom, and the king was still not there.

Later in the day, a small child was skipping over the drawbridge and noticed something strange. There beside the drawbridge where the first great stone was laid, the child saw a great big hole. The great stone was gone.

They say if you travel down that road there, not that one, over there, and go over the hill and across the valley, you will come to a crossroads.

They say at the crossroads sits a man with pleasant eyes and an easy smile sitting on a great stone.

The End

No Cupcakes

Stephanie Remington
April 2020

S arah came home from school on Tuesday and said to her mommy, "Mommy, tomorrow is my birthday, and I want to bring a special treat for my class."

"Okay, Sarah, what would you like to bring? Would you like to make cupcakes?" Sarah's mother asked her.

"But, Mom, everyone makes cupcakes. I want something special. Something super that everyone will love. I want it to be the best thing that anyone ever brought for their birthday," Sarah told her mother.

Sarah's mother smiled at her nicely and said, "But, honey, everyone loves cupcakes."

Sarah put her hands on hips and said, "No cupcakes!"

"Then what do you want to make?" Sarah's mom asked.

Sarah thought. And she thought. And she thought some more. But she could not think of anything to make.

"I bet Daddy will know what to make," Sarah thought as she ran out of the room into her dad's study.

She walked right up to her father and said, "Daddy, tomorrow is my birthday, and I want to bring a special treat for my class. I want to make something special. Something super that everyone will love. I want it to be the best thing that anyone ever brought for their birthday, but I do not know what to make."

"Why do you not make cupcakes? Everyone loves cupcakes," Sarah's father answered her.

"No cupcakes!" Sarah said.

Then what do you want to make?" asked her father

Sarah did not know, so she decided to ask her big brother, Cory. He would surely know what to make. After all, he has had a lot of birthdays.

She marched right up to her brother, who was watching TV, and said, "Cory, tomorrow is my birthday, and I want to bring a special treat for my class. I want to make something special. Something super that everyone will love. I want it to be the best thing that anyone ever brought for their birthday, but I do not know what to make."

"Why do you not make cupcakes? Everyone loves cupcakes," Cory said as he pushed her aside so he could see the TV.

"No cupcakes!" Sarah said.

"Then what are you going to make?" Cory asked.

Sarah had no idea what to make, so she went to the neighbour's house and knocked on the door. When Mrs. Pither answered, Sarah said, "Mrs. Pither, tomorrow is my birthday, and I want to bring a special treat for my class. I want to make something special. Something super that everyone will love. I want it to be the best thing that anyone ever brought for their birthday, but I do not know what to make."

"What about cupcakes?" Mrs. Pither said, "Everyone loves cupcakes."

"No cupcakes!" Sarah said.

Sarah went back to her house and into her room and thought. She thought and thought and thought. She thought until it felt like her brain was going to melt. Then she thought some more.

I know, Sarah thought, *I can make peanut butter bars.*

"But wait, Toby is allergic to peanuts."

So Sarah thought some more.

"I could bring ice cream, but it would melt before I got to school."

It was almost suppertime and still Sarah did not know what to make. After supper, she thought some more. Finally, Sarah decided what to make.

The next day at school, the teacher said, "Sarah, it is your birthday. Did you bring anything for the class?"

Sarah smiled and said, "I brought cupcakes ! Everyone loves cupcakes!"

And it was true. Everyone enjoyed the cupcakes that Sarah brought.

The End

Squiggly, Wiggly, and Jonathan Thomas Henry

P. Kevin Remington
March 2020

I would like to tell you a story about three friends of mine. They lived out behind my shed in the backyard. Their names are Squiggly, Wiggly, and Jonathan Thomas Henry, and they are worms.

Now Squiggly and Wiggly are regular worms, but their friend, Jonathan Thomas Henry, is a wee bit different. He would wear a fedora to school and a little wormy knapsack. Jonathan Thomas Henry did not do regular wormy things. Though Jonathan Thomas Henry is a bit different, Squiggly, Wiggly, and Jonathan Thomas Henry are the best of friends.

Let me tell you the story of how the three worms became great friends.

Jonathan Thomas Henry was the new worm at school. He went to school, like all the other worms. He would ride his worm bike down the street. He played in the water from the hose. He went to Worm Scouts.

Still Jonathan Thomas Henry was a bit different. He wore a hat, a fedora. Most worms do not wear hats.

The three worms were not always the best of friends.

One day, Squiggly was out playing down by the hose where the water trickles out by the yard. He was having great fun splashing in and out and in and out and in and out of the water as worms tend to do. After a little while, his friend, Wiggly, came to play with him.

Little did they know that high above them, way up in the sky, was a robin watching them. The robin flew around and around, just waiting for the right time to snatch these two juicy worms. Squiggly and Wiggly did not see the robin and just kept on playing in the water having fun.

When Squiggly and Wiggly noticed the shadow above them, it was too late. The robin swooped down and grabbed Squiggly and flew him way up into the air. The robin flew Squiggly high into a tree almost five feet into the air and dropped him on branch to eat him later.

Squiggly was up in the tree, and he was scared. He had never been in a tree before. He had never been so high up in his whole life. He was terrified. He was in tears. He knew that he was going to be eaten by the robin.

Wiggly was very scared. He did not know what to do. He ran to the tree. He ran to the hose. He ran back to the tree. He ran back to the hose. He did not know what to do. In the distance, Wiggly saw Jonathan Thomas Henry, and he ran to tell what had happened and see if Jonathan Thomas Henry knew what to do.

Wiggly said, "Jonathan, Jonathan, Jonathan!"

Jonathan Thomas Henry said, "What? What? What?"

Wiggly then told him that a robin had taken Squiggly and put him high in a tree and was going to eat him. Wiggly said, "I do not know what to do. Do you?"

Jonathan Thomas Henry was a Worm Scout. Worm Scouts are always prepared. He ran to the tree and looked up. Squiggly was way up there. Squiggly was almost five feet off the ground, and that is really high for a worm, but Jonathan Thomas Henry knew exactly what to do.

Jonathan Thomas Henry started squeezing up between the ridges on the rough bark of the tree. He climbed over the branches. After a long time, Jonathan Thomas Henry finally got up to the branch that Squiggly was on sitting on.

Jonathan Thomas Henry was so happy. He thought he could now save Squiggly and the two of them could climb down the same way he climbed up.

He said, "Squiggly, come over here so we can climb down." Squiggly was too scared to move. Squiggly held on to the branch for dear life, and he was not about to move and fall climbing down the tree.

Jonathan Thomas Henry had a problem. He had to get Squiggly to climb down. He knew that he could climb down, but he could not get Squiggly to climb down. How was he to rescue Squiggly now?

Jonathan Thomas Henry thought and thought. He knew the robin could return any time and fly there and get both of them. Then Jonathan Thomas Henry had an idea. If the robin can fly, so can they.

Jonathan Thomas Henry said, "Squiggly, if you will not climb down, we will have to fly down."

"What!" squeaked Squiggly.

Jonathan Thomas Henry took Squiggly to the end of the branch,and there was a nice big green leaf. Jonathan Thomas Henry climbed on the leaf and told Squiggly to climb on with him.

Squiggly cried, "I do not see how we are going to fly. The robin is going to come and eat us both!"

Jonathan Thomas Henry said "No, no, no," and he took off his knapsack. Then he took out his Worm Scout knife, and he started cutting the leaf from the branch. After a few minutes of cutting the leaf, Jonathan Thomas Henry put Worm Scout knife back in his knapsack and broke the last piece, and the leaf started to fall free.

The leaf floated on the air a little over here. A little over there. Squiggly and Jonathan Thomas Henry floated gently down to the ground on the back of the leaf.

Jonathan Thomas Henry was having a marvelous time and whooping and laughing. Squiggly was holding on for dear life and was terrified.

Suddenly, just as the leaf was about six inches above the ground, a gust of wind grabbed the leaf and flipped it over. Jonathan Thomas Henry and Squiggly both fell to the ground with a thump!

Squiggly was so surprised that he was still alive.

Jonathan Thomas Henry burst out laughing and laughing and laughing. Then Squiggly started laughing. When Wiggly rushed over to see if they were okay. They all were laughing. It was a long time before Jonathan Thomas Henry and Squiggly were able to tell Wiggly what had happened.

From that day forward, Squiggly, Wiggly, and Jonathan Thomas Henry were the best of friends.

The End

Grandpa's Tea

P. Kevin Remington
June 2020

I would like to tell you a story about my three friends. They are three worms that live out behind my shed in the backyard. Squiggly, Wiggly, and Jonathan Thomas Henry and they are good friends.

Now Squiggly and Wiggly were just your normal sort of worms, but their friend, Jonathan Thomas Henry, was a wee bit different for a worm. Jonathan Thomas Henry always carried a little wormy knapsack, and he always wore a fedora. A very strange hat for a worm to wear, but he always wore a fedora. Squiggly and Wiggly still liked Jonathan Thomas Henry because they were best friends.

One day, the three friends were in the school yard at recess time, and Squiggly and Wiggly and Jonathan Thomas Henry were talking about their grandparents.

Wiggly was saying, "I got to go see my grandpa this weekend. I hate seeing Grandpa. He always pinches my cheek. He always gives me a hug. He always smells like camomile tea! Yuck! I hate going to visit Grandpa!"

Jonathan Thomas Henry said, "Really? I always love going to see my grandpa."

Wiggly asked, "Why? Isn't he awful?"

"Oh no," said Jonathan Thomas Henry. "My grandpa is a wonderful fellow. He was a carpenter. He built houses and stores. You know that big slide down by the compost heap, he worked on that and helped built it. When I went to visit him, he would show me all his tools and tell me how they were used."

Jonathan Thomas Henry went on, "When we were in his workshop, he would tell me stories and secrets. He would tell me about when Dad was a little worm and all the secrets he caught Dad doing. And they were really good secrets! Then Grandpa would have Grandma make cookies just for me. Though I do think Grandpa ate most of the cookies. *And* every day at three o'clock exactly, he would stop what he was doing. He would go get cleaned up, and him and Grandma would have tea. They would have Earl Grey tea every day at three. Grandpa would sometimes pick me up and take me to have tea with him and Grandma."

Then Jonathan Thomas Henry explained, "My grandpa died a year or two ago. I miss him. I miss his stories. I miss him showing me things. I miss the secrets."

When he had finished talking, Jonathan Thomas Henry had painted a beautiful picture of his grandfather.
Wiggly was not really convinced about how good it was to visit Grandpa.

So Squiggly also told a story about his grandpa.

Squiggly started telling his story, "My grandma would make the best cookies. And every day at four, Grandma would put aside two cookies for Grandpa. When I went to visit them, Grandma would put aside two cookies for me and two cookies for Grandpa. Every day at four, we would stop and have cookies and milk."

Wiggly started thinking that this does not sound like his grand-parents at all. This is very strange. Jonathan Thomas Henry and Squiggly both liked their grandparents.

Jonathan Thomas Henry suggested to Wiggly, "Go talk with your grandpa. Find out why he likes camomile tea. Better yet, why not have some camomile tea with him?"

The next weekend, Wiggly went to visit his grandparents
Wiggly talked with his grandfather.
Wiggly had tea with his grandfather.
On Monday at school during recess, Wiggly had all sorts of stories about his grandpa to tell Squiggly and Jonathan Thomas Henry.

With great excitement, Wiggly said, "My grandfather was an engineer. We had tea. I now like camomile tea."

Wiggly told his friends all sorts of things that he learned from his grandpa.

Squiggly, Wiggly, and Jonathan Thomas Henry always had the best stories to tell about their grandparents and loved tea and cookies.

The End

Monsters under the Bed

P. Kevin Remington
May 2020

I would like to tell you a story about my three friends, Squiggly, Wiggly, and Jonathan Thomas Henry, and the monster under the bed.

Squiggly, Wiggly, and Jonathan Thomas Henry are three best-friends. They are three worms that live out behind my shed in the backyard.

Now Squiggly and Wiggly were just your normal sort of worms, but their friend, Jonathan Thomas Henry, was a wee bit odd for a worm. As an example, he liked to wear a hat, called a fedora, and wear a little wormy knapsack. No worms, that I know, wear a fedora and a knapsack except Jonathan Thomas Henry.

One day, Squiggly, Wiggly, and Jonathan Thomas Henry were talking about the monsters that live under the bed. Everyone knows that monsters live under the bed.

Squiggly had a solution to protect him from the monsters under the bed. His parents told him the monster words that keep monsters away. This worked for Squiggly. Every time he said the monster words, it would keep monsters away from under his bed. In fact, these words worked for both monsters and giraffes. Ever since Squiggly had said the monster words, he has never seen a giraffe under his bed, but he was not taking any chances and was always careful to say the words.

Squiggly's monster words were, "Booga! Booga! Booga!"

Wiggly was also very concerned about the monsters under his bed. However, Wiggly's parents got him the monster juice. If you spray a little monster juice under your bed, the monsters can not live there. Each night after Wiggly got tucked into bed, he would spray a little monster juice under his bed. There has not been a single monster under his bed since he sprayed the monster juice. The monster juice smells a little bit like vinegar and apples, but that is okay because it works.

Jonathan Thomas Henry has a problem. He knows that there is a monster under his bed. He knows that if he is not careful to keep from slipping out of the covers at night, the monster will get him.

Jonathan Thomas Henry told his father about the monster under his bed.

His father said, "There is no such thing as monsters. Go to bed.

Each night, Jonathan Thomas Henry's father would read him a story. Then he would tuck him in. Then he would turn on Jonathan Thomas Henry's night-light, kiss him good night, leave, and close the door.

But each night after his father left his bedroom, Jonathan Thomas Henry would reach into his knapsack and get out his extendable pokey stick from Worm Scouts. He would extend the stick as far as it would go, which was almost two inches long. Then he would sweep it under his bed to make sure there were no monsters. Still, Jonathan Thomas Henry thought there was a monster under his bed.

Squiggly suggested that Jonathan Thomas Henry try the monster words. After all, the words work for Squiggly, so they should work for Jonathan Thomas Henry.

The next night, Jonathan Thomas Henry's father read him a story. Then he tucked him in. Then he turned on Jonathan Thomas Henry's night-light, kissed him good night, left, and closed the door.

This night, before he went to sleep, Jonathan Thomas Henry said the monster words, "Booga! Booga! Booga!"

Jonathan Thomas Henry was not sure if the words worked. He still got out his pokey stick and swept it under his bed and then went to sleep.

The next day at school, Wiggly said, "I can give you some of my monster juice. That will keep your monster away."

The next night, Jonathan Thomas Henry's father read him a story. Then he tucked him in. Then he turned on Jonathan Thomas Henry's night-light, kissed him good night, left, and closed the door.

This night, before he went to sleep, Jonathan Thomas Henry sprayed the monster juice under the bed. It did smell like vinegar and apple, and he was still certain that there was a monster under his bed. He still got out his pokey stick and swept it under his bed and did not feel anything, so he went to sleep.

The next day at school, Jonathan Thomas Henry told Squiggly and Wiggly that nothing worked. He was sure that there was still a monster under his bed.

Squiggly said, "Why do you not look under the bed? Just to see if there really is a monster."

Jonathan Thomas Henry was shocked and said, "What if there is a monster? What if he eats me?"

Wiggly said, "He might be friendly."

"Really?" said Jonathan Thomas Henry.

"Really!" said Squiggly and Wiggly together.

That night, Jonathan Thomas Henry thought, *I am going to look under the bed. I am going to see if there really is a monster living there.*

That night, Jonathan Thomas Henry's father read him a story. Then he tucked him in. Then he turned on Jonathan Thomas Henry's night-light, kissed him good night, left, and closed the door.

This night, before he went to sleep, Jonathan Thomas Henry reached for his knapsack. And instead of pulling out his Worm Scout pokey stick, he pulled out his Worm Scout flashlight. He crawled out of bed and looked under the bed. He did not see anything. He turned on his flashlight, and he looked under the bed. He still did not see anything. Then Jonathan Thomas Henry crawled under the bed, and there in the back corner where it is always dark, he shone his flashlight, and there was the monster!

Oh my goodness, Jonathan Thomas Henry was scared!

Then he looked closer. Then he looked even closer still, and he saw that the monster that scared him so much was just a cricket.

Jonathan Thomas Henry said, "Hello!"

The cricket said, "Hello!"

Jonathan Thomas Henry was curious now and asked, "Do you live under my bed?"

The cricket replied, "Yes, it is a very nice bed."

"My name is Jonathan Thomas Henry, what is yours?" inquired Jonathan Thomas Henry.

"Larry," said the cricket.

"You are Larry, and you live under my bed," said Jonathan Thomas Henry. "Are the any more monsters under my bed?"

"Oh, I have never seen a monster under the bed," said Larry, "Just me."

Jonathan Thomas Henry was still curious and asked, "What do you do during the daytime when I go to school?"

Larry said, "I go to cricket school."

Then Jonathan Thomas Henry and Larry had a very nice chat. It seemed that Larry did have one problem. He did not like the night-light.

The next night, Jonathan Thomas Henry's father read him a story. Then he tucked him in. Then he turned on the night-light, but Jonathan Thomas Henry said that he did not need the night-light any more.

His father asked, "But, what about the monsters?"

Jonathan Thomas Henry said, "There are no monsters under my bed, just a cricket named Larry."

Jonathan Thomas Henry's father kissed him good night, left, and closed the door and never turned on the night-light again.

Squiggly, Wiggly, and Jonathan Thomas Henry all agreed that there were no monsters under their beds.

The End

The Great Camping Adventure

P. Kevin Remington
June 2020

I would like to tell you a story about my three friends Squiggly, Wiggly, and Jonathan Thomas Henry. Squiggly, Wiggly, and Jonathan Thomas Henry are three best friends. They are three worms that live out behind my shed in the backyard.

Now Squiggly and Wiggly were just your normal sort of worms, but their friend, Jonathan Thomas Henry, was a wee bit odd for a worm. As an example, he liked to wear a hat, called a fedora, and wear a little wormy knapsack. No worms, that I know, wear a fedora and a knapsack except Jonathan Thomas Henry.

One day, Squiggly, Wiggly, and Jonathan Thomas Henry decided that they would go camping.

Jonathan Thomas Henry's father said that since they are just little worms, they could put up a tent in Jonathan Thomas Henry's backyard, and they could camp there.

"Hurray!" shouted Squiggly, Wiggly, and Jonathan Thomas Henry. "What a great idea!"

That night after the tent was pitched, all three of the worms got their camping gear, Worm Scout sleeping bags, and Worm Scout flashlights. It was just going to be Squiggly, Wiggly, Jonathan Thomas Henry, and Larry the cricket.

Larry is a cricket who lives under Jonathan Thomas Henry's bed. Jonathan Thomas Henry thought Larry was a monster, but he was just a cricket. The three friends thought it would be very polite to invite Larry do join them camping. Larry had his own cricket sleeping bag.

That night, as the boys were all settling down, Jonathan Thomas Henry's mother brought out camping snacks. They had little chocolate bars, s'mores, gummie grubs, and rice crispy squares.

It was getting later in the evening, and as it was getting dark, Jonathan Thomas Henry turned on his Worm Scout flashlight, and they all settled into their sleeping bags. After everyone was settled, the time was just right to tell stories. Every camping trip has a time when you tell stories, and this camping trip was no different.

Squiggly told the first story. It was about being captured and taken high up into a tree. It was a great adventure story.

The next story told was by Wiggly. He told the story about his grandfather and how he was an engineer and all the adventure he had.

When it was Jonathan Thomas Henry's turn to tell a story, it was a very scary story. It was about the worm that turned!

Larry, not to be left out, told the story about the great white cricket. The great white cricket only comes out at night and only on very stormy nights. You have to be very careful that the great white cricket does not get you late at night in a storm.

Oh, it was the scariest story.

After the stories were told, they all settled back to get some sleep. Outside the tent, they could hear the wind blowing and howling. *Whooosh, whoosh.* It was just the wind.

Then the leaves started to make a sound as the wind blew them in the trees. *Swhooshy, swhooshy!* But that was just leaves, so everyone thought everything was still okay.

Jonathan Thomas Henry said, "Do not worry. Everything is fine." He left his flashlight on, and Squiggly, Wiggly, and Larry turned on their flashlights too.

Now the birds started to make a noise outside their tent. They heard an owl whooing and some small birds chittering.

Jonathan Thomas Henry said, "That is just birds. Everything is fine."

Everything was fine, but the boys could not fall asleep. Then the rain started to fall. It plinked and plunked on the tent and made a terrible noise.

Suddenly, there was a loud boom of thunder and a bright flash of lightning that made the inside of the tent look like a bright sunny day for only a moment. Then the tent went back to the gloomy light of just the flashlights.

Jonathan Thomas Henry said in his bravest, quivering voice, "It is okay, everyone. That is just a storm, and we are safe here in the tent."

Soon, the storm passed. Everyone had finally fallen asleep.

In the morning, Squiggly and Wiggly were sound asleep snuggly on the floor in Jonathan Thomas Henry's bedroom. Jonathan Thomas Henry was snug safely in his bed. And Larry was in his corner under the bed.

That was the end of Squiggly, Wiggly, Jonathan Thomas Henry, and Larry's great camping adventure.

The End

Squiggly, Wiggly, Jonathan Thomas Henry, and Orville

P. Kevin Remington
August 2020

I would like to tell you a story about three friends of mine. They lived out behind my shed in the backyard. Their names are Squiggly, Wiggly, and Jonathan Thomas Henry, and they are worms.

Now Squiggly and Wiggly are regular worms, but their friend, Jonathan Thomas Henry, is a wee bit different. He would wear a fedora to school and a little wormy knapsack. Jonathan Thomas Henry did not do regular wormy things. Though Jonathan Thomas Henry is a bit different, Squiggly, Wiggly, and Jonathan Thomas Henry are the best of friends.

Let me tell you the story about Squiggly, Wiggly, Jonathan Thomas Henry, and Orville.

Jonathan Thomas Henry was a Worm Scout. Squiggly and Wiggly were Worm Scouts also, and the three of them went to Worm Scout meetings every Monday. Every Monday, Squiggly's father would pick up the three worms and take them to Worm Scouts.

Jonathan Thomas Henry lived down the street and around the corner. Every Monday evening, he would rush out to the corner where they would pick him up. He did not want to be late and make them wait for him, so he rushed out there early and sat on top of the mailbox on the corner. Jonathan Thomas Henry would just sit there waiting for Squiggly's father to come and pick him up.

As Jonathan Thomas Henry sat on the mailbox, the sun would set, and the stars would start to shine. Jonathan Thomas Henry would see the first and brightest star in the sky.

Jonathan Thomas Henry would say to himself, "There is my friend up in the sky shining bright."

After a while, Jonathan Thomas Henry thought his friend, in the sky, should have a name. He was quite certain the star had a name, but Jonathan Thomas Henry did not know the name, so he called him Orville.

This week when Squiggly, Wiggly, and Jonathan Thomas Henry were at the Worm Scout meeting, there was gentleman there to tell them all about the stars and constellations and their proper names.

They learned about the Big Dipper. The Big Dipper had lots names, such as Ursa Major, which mean the Big Bear. It was also called Charles's Wagon. That seemed very strange to the three boys, but it seems it was German and a fellow named Charles had a wagon. It was also called, the Wagon, the Plow, and it all depended on where you lived on what name is used.

People who lived in Europe, North America, China, and Russia, they all saw the same stars and constellations, and all called them by different names.

Squiggly, Wiggly, and Jonathan Thomas Henry were learning about the Big Dipper, Little Dipper, Orion, and Cassiopeia who used to be a queen but now just looks like a *W* in the sky.

Jonathan Thomas Henry was paying close attention to everything the gentleman was telling him about the stars in the sky. Jonathan Thomas Henry thought this man may know the name of the bright star in the sky that he named Orville.

After Jonathan Thomas Henry asked the gentleman, he replied, "Oh, that might be the North Star, which is also called Polaris. Or it could just be a planet. Venus is very bright in the early evening sky and reflects the sun's light and looks like a star."

Jonathan Thomas Henry thought about what the gentleman had said. He did not like the answer. Jonathan Thomas Henry thought that every Monday evening, he would sit on the mailbox waiting to be picked up by Squiggly's father. And every Monday evening as he was waiting, his star friend would appear in the sky and wait with him. No, that would be rude to just call him the North Star or Venus. No, his name is Orville, and he is Jonathan Thomas Henry's friend.

Jonathan Thomas Henry chatted with Squiggly and Wiggly. They talked and talked and decided that since the Big Dipper can have many names and the Little Dipper can have many names and Cassiopeia can be the Lady in a chair or a *W*, the first bright light in the sky on a Monday evening can have the name Orville.

From that moment on, each time evening was coming and twilight was settling, Jonathan Thomas Henry, Squiggly, and Wiggly, would look for the bright light and say, "Hello, Orville."

All the other stars would come out, bright and sparkly, but they knew Orville was their friend.

Jonathan Thomas Henry had one more problem, the moon. Jupiter, Saturn, Mars, Neptune, and Uranus all had a bunch of moons, and they all had names. Why did the one and only moon around the Earth not have a name? But that is a story for another time.

The End

Wiggly's Birthday

P. Kevin Remington
May 2020

I would like to tell you a story about my three friends, Squiggly, Wiggly, and Jonathan Thomas Henry. Squiggly, Wiggly, and Jonathan Thomas Henry are three best friends. They are three worms that live out behind my shed in the backyard.

Now Squiggly and Wiggly were just your normal sort of worms, but their friend, Jonathan Thomas Henry, was a wee bit odd for a worm. As an example, he liked to wear a hat, called a fedora, and wear a little wormy knapsack to keep things in. No worms, that I know, wear a fedora and a knapsack except Jonathan Thomas Henry.

Today was going to be a really great day. Today was Wiggly's birthday.

Wiggly jumped out of bed. He rushed downstairs to the breakfast table. He sat there with a big smile on his face, and nothing happened. His mother had his breakfast of toasted grubs ready. Worms really like toasted grubs. His father said good morning. Nobody wished him a happy birthday or patted him on the back or anything.

Perhaps they just forgot, thought Wiggly. *They will remember and do something later.*

So Wiggly went to school. He went down the street, and he went by Mr. Stone's house. Mr. Stone was working in his garden, and all you could see was his back. Mr. Stone always worked in his garden but each day he would smile at Wiggly, wave, and say hello. Today, all you could see was Mr. Stone's back. He did not wave or smile or anything. Wiggly thought that was very strange.

Wiggly continued on his way to school and met up with his friends, Squiggly and Jonathan Thomas Henry.

Another strange thing happened. On birthdays, Jonathan Thomas Henry always tips his hat to the birthday person. Today, Jonathan Thomas Henry did not tip his hat to Wiggly. They just went on their way to school. Wiggly thought it was perhaps he just forgot and will do it later.

When the three friends arrived at school, everyone was out in the yard playing. They were playing Wiggly's favourite game, Turn the Worm. Wiggly is very good at Turn the Worm. When the bell rang to go to class, everyone went inside, but nobody had wished Wiggly a happy birthday. He was sure everyone knew it was Wiggly's birthday but still no happy greetings.

Mrs. Grub, the teacher, started teaching. As she was teaching, Wiggly thought this was strange. Usually when it is someone's birthday, Mrs. Grub has the whole class sing "Happy Birthday" to that person. Nobody was singing happy birthday to Wiggly, and he was starting to get a little bit sad.

When lunch came, Wiggly was a little bit happier. He knew that they would remember his birthday at a lunch. Jonathan Thomas Henry always carried a surprise for the birthday person in his knapsack. When it was Susie's birthday, Jonathan Thomas Henry gave her a spiced grub. When it was John's birthday, he gave him a little bit of a sliced apple which was really tasty.

Lunch came and went. Jonathan Thomas Henry did not give anything to Wiggly.

Wiggly was starting to get sad. Nobody wished him a happy birthday. Nobody tipped their hat to him. Nobody gave him anything special. Nobody remembered his birthday.

After school, the three friends walked down the street like they did every day.

Squiggly and Jonathan Thomas Henry then said "Goodbye!" and they left. They did not even stay to play.

Wiggly thought that was very strange, so he went home all by himself.

When Wiggly got home, there was nobody there. There was just a note that said, "Supper is in the oven, wormy pizza." Wiggly ate a slice of wormy pizza. He sat down and did his homework. As Wiggly was about to go to bed, he heard a noise in the backyard. He went to see what was making the sound. Nobody was home, so there should be no noise in the backyard.

Wiggly looked through the house, and nobody was home. When he looked in the backyard, he heard a very loud "Surprise !" There was everyone.

There was Squiggly and Jonathan Thomas Henry. Mr. Stone and Mrs. Grub were there. Mom and Dad were there. There was a big sign that read "Happy Birthday Wiggly!" across the whole backyard. Everyone had gotten together to make this the biggest surprise birthday ever.

Wiggly was so happy.

Then Wiggly saw that there in the middle of the backyard, just waiting for him, was a giant birthday cake. It was three layers tall with a candle on the top for him to blow out.

This was the best birthday Wiggly had ever had with the best surprise ever!

The End

Christmas Slime

P. Kevin Remington
May 2020

I would like to tell you a story about my three friends, Squiggly, Wiggly, and Jonathan Thomas Henry. Squiggly, Wiggly, and Jonathan Thomas Henry are three best friends. They are three worms that live out behind my shed in the backyard.

Now Squiggly and Wiggly were just your normal sort of worms, but their friend, Jonathan Thomas Henry, was a wee bit odd for a worm. As an example, he liked to wear a hat, called a fedora, and wear a little wormy knapsack. No worms, that I know, wear a fedora and a knapsack except Jonathan Thomas Henry.

Jonathan Thomas Henry loved Christmas. He loved Christmas so much that he would even change his hat from a fedora to a touque. It was a nice red Christmas touque with a white trim and a white tassel at the top.

Wiggly loved to sing in the Christmas choir. Wiggly has a beautiful voice. In fact, he would sing wherever he went. His favourite Christmas carol was "Keep Warm, Under the Compost Heap." Any time you saw Wiggly during the Christmas season, you could be sure that he would be singing "Keep warm, under the compost heap!" over and over. Jonathan Thomas Henry and Squiggly would plead with Wiggly to sing a different Christmas carol, but that was the one Wiggly liked to sing.

Squiggly loved Christmas most of all. He loved everything that went with Christmas, music, bells, lights all around the town, and all the doorways aglow with Christmas glitter. Squiggly wrote a letter to Santa, the Krisworm, to find out what he was going to get for Christmas this year. And Squiggly wrote a letter to tell Krisworm where he lived so he would not be missed. And Squiggly wrote a letter to tell Krisworm where Wiggly and Jonathan Thomas Henry lived so they would not get missed. And Squiggly wrote a letter to tell Krisworm that he would put the very best apples right at the door for him to find on Christmas Eve.

Now my three friends go to school every day, but one day, just a little while before Christmas, Squiggly was very sad. He talked with Wiggly and Jonathan Thomas Henry at recess, and he told them, "My dad got a new job down at the compost heap. We have to move. I will have to go to a new school. I won't be able to play at the mall or the dirt hill. It is just a week before Christmas, and Santa won't know where I live. I don't have time to write a letter to tell Krisworm where my family moved. I am not going to get any Christmas slime at all this year."

Jonathan Thomas Henry and Wiggly were really concerned about this. Squiggly really loved Christmas, and it just seems so unfair.

Everyone went home that day.

Jonathan Thomas Henry called Wiggly. They talked and talked and did not know what to do. They wanted to do something for Squiggly.

The next day at school, Squiggly was much happier, and he said, "Hey, guys, I do not have to go to a new school. My dad just moved us down the street two blocks so that he is closer to the compost heap and I still get to go to the same school."

Then Squiggly started getting a bit sadder as he said, "But Krisworm won't be able to find me this year. I won't have time to tell him where we moved. But you guys have a good Christmas!"

Christmas was on Monday, and Jonathan Thomas Henry and Wiggly were very sad for Squiggly.

On the weekend before Christmas at Squiggly's new house, all the boxes were being unpacked. All the bags were being unpacked. There just was not any Christmas glow around the door. There were no Christmas lights anywhere. It just seemed that there was no time for Christmas.

Christmas Day came as it would each year. As the light was just starting to brighten the day, Squiggly could just see the light sliding into his bedroom window, and there were sparkles.

Sparkles?

That was very strange. As the sun shone brighter and filled Squiggly's bedroom, the whole room was just a glow with Christmas slime. There was Christmas slime on the ceiling. There was Christmas slime on the floor. There was Christmas slime all over the walls. There was Christmas slime on his bed. There was Christmas slime everywhere.

"Mom, Dad, the Krisworm made it here! I got Christmas slimed!" shouted Squiggly as he jumped out of bed and ran to the kitchen.

When Squiggly got to the kitchen, he noticed that there was no Christmas slime in the kitchen. In fact, there was no Christmas slime anywhere in the house, just his room. That was amazing.

Squiggly had an amazing Christmas.

On that same Christmas morning when Jonathan Thomas Henry and Wiggly woke up, the sun crept into their bedrooms. Through the windows, the bright morning light shone, but there was no sparkle. There was no Christmas slime in either of their bedrooms. There was Christmas slime all through the rest of their houses, but there was none in their bedrooms.

On Christmas Eve, Jonathan Thomas Henry and Wiggly had their moms and dads move their Christmas slime from their bedrooms to Squiggly's bedroom.

Everyone had a very Merry Christmas.

The End

Joe Cuervo

P. Kevin Remington
Abril 2020

There once was a little boy named Kyle who would walk to school every day. He would walk one block down the street, then left two blocks to the traffic light, then one more block to the school.

Every day, Kyle would leave his house and walk that one block down the street, and every day, he would see a big crow sitting up on the light standard.

Every day, Kyle would see the big crow and say, "Good morning!" Then he would walk off to school. When he was walking, he would mutter to himself because Kyle did not like school.

Every day, Kyle would mutter, "I do not like school. School is no fun. I want to play. School is for the birds!"

One morning, when Kyle left his house and he walked down the first block, he saw the big crow.

Kyle said, "Good morning!"

That morning, something different happened.

The crow answered back and said, "Why do you say school is for the birds? I am a bird. Perhaps I should come to the school and see."

Kyle was shocked. He had never had any bird talk to him before, and the big crow talked to him. Kyle thought about what the crow had said and thought this would be a good idea.

The big crow flew down beside Kyle, but Kyle said, "I cannot just take you to school. You are a bird, and they do not just let birds in to the school."

Kyle had an idea. He had his gym clothes in his knapsack, and he took out an extra T-shirt and put it over the crow. It fit perfectly. Then Kyle put his ball cap on the crow. It fit perfectly too. Then Kyle pulled out his gym sneakers from his knapsack and put them on the crow. They did not fit at all, so he put them back in his knapsack.

Since the crow was all dressed for school and Kyle had everything else back in his knapsack, the two of them walked off to school.

The crow then asked, "What is going to happen at school? What do they teach you?"

Kyle replied that they teach all sorts of things, like arithmetic, spelling, geography, and all sort of things that they think children should know.

When they got to Kyle's classroom, the teacher asked, "Who is this with you, Kyle?"

Kyle answered, "This is my cousin who is visiting."

The teacher told them to sit in the back of the class today. After Kyle and the crow were seated, the teacher took attendance. She called out everyone's name, and when she got to Kyle, she asked him to introduce his cousin to the class.

Kyle had to think quickly, and he said, "This is Joe Crow. He is a cousin and a very good friend of mine. He is just visiting." Kyle went on explaining.

"Welcome to the class," said the teacher.

Then the class started. They started with spelling and learning to spell words, like bus, train, and other vehicles that moved on wheels. Then the class started learning about arithmetic.

They learned that 1+1 = 2. They learned that 2+2 = 4. They learned that when you divide 9 by 3, you get 3.

The crow was pondering all these things that they were learning. He thought to himself, *This is very strange. I have lived a long time and never had to know that 1+1 = 2.* The crow was starting to get bewildered.

The next subject was going to be social studies. They were going to learn about airplanes and flying, but first, it was recess time.

Well, all the kids went outside to play, and Kyle and Joe went to play too. They went on the swings. They ran around. They played dodgeball. Joe was really good at dodgeball because he did not get hit even once. Then recess was over, and all the kids went back to class, and Kyle and Joe went with them.

After they sat down, Joe thought recess was pretty good for school, but he was not sure about the other stuff.

When social studies started, the teacher started talking about airplanes and big wings.

Joe was very interested because Joe was a crow, and he had wings.

Then the teacher talked about engines and how the engines pushed the plane forward.

Joe was a crow and did not have an engine, he just sort of jumped forward and flapped his wings.

Then the teacher talked about lift plus thrust equals drag, and Joe was very confused. Joe did not know what they were talking about. The teacher went on to explain large plane and small planes and planes that just glided in the air.

Finally, Joe had enough. He jumped up on the desk and said, *"Squawk!"*

The teacher jumped up on her desk and said, "Yikes! What was that?"

And Joe said *"Squawk!"* again.

The teacher looked at Joe and said, "That is not a boy, that is a crow!"

Joe, the crow, said, "That is not how you fly. You spread your wings and you jump and you flap your wings. If you want to turn, you flap your wings this way. If you want to turn that way, you flap your wings that way. And if you want to land, you just move your feathers gently."

The whole class was shocked, and the teacher did not know what to say.

Joe Crow took off his ball cap and the T-shirt, and he spread his wings and jumped and flapped and flew right out the window.

From that day on, Kyle would leave his house in the morning to walk to school. He would walk one block and see the big crow on the lamp standard.

Kyle would always say, "Good morning!"

Only now the crow would always reply, "School is not for the birds. It is for little boys like you. Off your go!"

And every day, Kyle went to school.

The End

The World's Greatest Magician

P. Kevin Remington
April 2020

Kevin was the world's greatest magician. In fact, Kevin was the world's most magnificent wizard. Kevin was so good that there wasn't going to be anybody better than him in all the world, ever. Kevin was only eight years old.

Do you know how Kevin knew he was the world's greatest magician? He was born to parents who were fantastic with magic.

Kevin's mother was a weather witch. His mother could make it rain for when the farmers need rain for their crops. When there was a bad storm, his mother could make it go out to sea where there were no ships, and all that happened would be a nice rain on the town.

Kevin's father was a very important wizard. His father could summon demons to help do great building. The demons would help to build great buildings, dams, and massive bridges. The demons would do the work that was too dangerous for people.

Because of his wonderful parents, Kevin just knew he was going to be a fantastic magician and the best wizard in the entire world. He was not going to be like his friend Erik's father. Erik's father was one of those stage magicians who made things disappear, cut ladies in half, and all that sort of thing. No, Kevin was going to be great! Just like his father.

Being as Kevin was going to be a great wizard, he thought he should practise. Kevin thought he should start out with something simple. Erik's father made things disappear, so it cannot be that difficult. Kevin decided that he would make things disappear.

Kevin had seen his father make things disappear, and he had seen Erik's father make things disappear. So Kevin got all the stuff together and set everything up just right in his bedroom. He knew all the right words. Kevin was ready to make things disappear.

Kevin set his stuffed dog in the middle of the floor. Kevin set the right stuff all round the stuffed dog. Kevin waved his hands above the stuff dog. Kevin said the magic words…and nothing happened.

Something must have been wrong, so Kevin did it all again… and nothing happened. Kevin decided that perhaps it does not work with stuffed dogs. Kevin got the family cat and set it right in the middle of the floor and did it all over again. Still nothing happened. In fact, Kevin tried it three times and still nothing happened.

Obviously, Kevin was doing something wrong. He decided that he will have to watch his father more carefully. As Kevin was about to leave his room, he noticed that the doorknob on his closet was missing. He thought that was very strange because he did not recall his mother or father taking the doorknob off his closet. As Kevin reached for this bedroom door, he noticed that the doorknob on his bedroom door was missing too! He thought this was very strange.

Kevin looked around the house and could not find the doorknobs anywhere. He had made the doorknobs disappear! He could not make the stuffed dog or the family cat disappear, but he could make doorknobs disappear. This is great! He should be able to make other things disappear.

Kevin set his school books in the middle of his bedroom. He did all the right stuff to make it disappear, and lo and behold, nothing happened. Well, almost nothing happened. The doorknob on the front door and the back door had disappeared.

Kevin looked everywhere for the missing doorknobs. He knew his mother and father would be upset to find all the doorknobs missing. Kevin looked and looked.

When Kevin's father got home, he noticed the doorknobs were missing. He knew just what Kevin had done.

His father said, "They cannot have gotten far, so let us go look and see where they wound up."

It was not until later in the day when they found all the doorknobs were at the bottom of the well in their backyard. Kevin's father got all the doorknobs out of the well and put them back on all the doors. Then he had a talk with Kevin.

"You should not play with magic," started Kevin's father. "You are not old enough to work with magic, so you must stop working magic until you are older."

Kevin was eight years old, and he thought he was plenty old enough to do magic.

The next day, Kevin decided to try something different. Now that he knows how to make something disappear, he will do something different. He just did not know what to do. He knew that he had school homework to do, but that did not sound like fun at all. In fact, Kevin had math homework, and math homework is hard. Kevin thought that since his father called demons to do the hard building work for people, Kevin would call a demon to do his hard math homework. Then he would get perfect in school.

Kevin got everything ready and set up just like his father. Kevin said the magic words. Kevin waved his hands, like his father, and *poof!* There was a demon. In fact, it was an arithmetic demon.

Kevin did not know much about arithmetic demons, but this one only did adding. Kevin would have to call a demon to do the subtracting. He would have to call a demon to do the dividing. He would have to call a demon to do the multiplying. Soon, his whole bedroom was full of demons, but his homework was all done.

The demons kept on working and did his math homework for the next night and the night after and the night after that. In fact, the demons did all the homework in the book, and Kevin did not know how to stop them or get rid of them. The problem was that Kevin had seen his father call demons, but he never saw how his father got rid of demons.

Kevin got all his magic stuff, and he said the words and waved his hands, and nothing worked. The demons just kept on doing arithmetic. Soon, they would be up to next year's math homework.

Kevin finally came up with a brilliant idea. He could not make the demons disappear, but he could make doorknobs disappear. Kevin set up all his magic stuff again. Then just before he said the words and waved his hands, he tied a rope from the doorknob on his closet to the demon. Then poof, the doorknob disappeared, and the demon disappeared.

This was a great solution. Kevin tied each demon to a doorknob and made them all disappear.

Unfortunately, Kevin had made his closet doorknob disappear. He made his bedroom doorknob disappear. He made the front door and back door doorknobs disappear. He even made his parents bedroom doorknob disappear. He did not have a demon for that one, but he was having fun making things disappear.

Now Kevin was happy. The demons were gone. His math homework was done. In fact, all his math homework for the whole year was done. Kevin decided that he would just watch a little TV until his parents came home.

When Kevin's parents got home, they noticed all the doorknobs were missing again. They were very upset.

They said, "Kevin, what did you do?"

Kevin said, "Nothing. I just did my homework."

Kevin's father asked, "Why are the doorknobs missing?"

Kevin answered that he got demons to help him with his arithmetic homework. He then explained that he did not know how to get rid of the demons, so he tied them to the doorknobs and made the doorknobs disappear and demons then with them.

Kevin's father shouted, "Yikes! You sent all those doorknobs to the bottom of the well with demons?"

They all ran out into the backyard to the well, and sure enough, there at the bottom of the well were all the doorknobs, and tied to each doorknob was a demon.

Kevin's father did his magic and made all the demons disappear. Then he put all the doorknobs back on all the doors. Then Kevin's mother and father made Kevin do all his math homework over again himself.

In fact, they made Kevin do all his homework himself and could not watch TV for a whole week.

Kevin never made any doorknobs disappear again.

The End

Linda y los Animales Peligrosos

P. Kevin Remington
July 2020

Linda lived with her mother and father in Terra Nova National Park in Newfoundland/Labrador. Linda's father worked for the park, and as such, they lived deep in the park. They lived 114 kilometers from anybody. Linda got to spend a lot of time in the woods playing by herself. Her parents would always warn Linda to be very careful in the woods because there were dangerous animals and she could get hurt.

Linda did not know what was a dangerous animal. In her comic books, she read about Queen Snakes and Gully Cats, and they were supposed to be very dangerous.

Every day, Linda would go out into the woods looking for Queen Snakes and Gully Cats.

One day, while looking for Queen Snakes and Gully Cats, Linda found that she wandered too far from home. It was getting dark, and she did not know the way home. She did not find any snakes or cats, but she did run into a moose.

The moose looked at Linda.

Linda looked at the moose.

The moose licked Linda all the way from her chin to the top of her head then picked her up by the scruff of her jacket and carried Linda home.

The next day, Linda went looking for Queen Snakes and Gully Cats again. Linda thought that if she found the snakes and cats, she could point them out to her mother and father, and they would know she would be safe.

Linda spent all day looking in the gullies and looking in the bushes and looking in the trees. She looked high and low. She looked here and there. She looked everywhere but did not notice where she was going.

Once again, it was getting dark, and Linda was lost. She had wandered too far from home, again. As she looked around the bend, she found a great big bear.

The bear looked at Linda.

Linda looked at the bear.

The bear then licked Linda all the way from her belly button to the top of her head, then it picked her up by the seat of her pants and carried Linda home.

The next day, Linda thought she had a plan so she could not get lost. She would search in circles around and around her house looking for Queen Snakes and Gully Cats. As the circles got larger and larger, Linda would always know how to go back to the middle of the circle.

Once again, it got dark. Once again, Linda got lost. It seems that when the circles are really big, you cannot find the middle. This time though, there was no moose to take her home. There was no bear to take her home. This time, she turned around a tree, and there were two coyotes.

The coyotes looked at Linda.

Linda looked at the coyotes.

The coyotes then licked Linda all over and grabbed her by her feet and dragged her home.

The next day, Linda was getting ready to go out searching again.

Her father saw her about to leave and asked, "Where are you going?"

Linda said, "I am going to look for dangerous animals. I have looked all around and have not found a single Queen Snake or Gully Cat." Linda continued, "In fact, I keep getting lost when I search. One day, a moose brought me home. The next day, a bear brought me home. Yesterday, two coyotes dragged me home."

Linda's mother and father said, "Yikes! Linda, those are dangerous animals!"

Linda replied, "No, they are not! They are my friends."

The End

Princess Stephanie and Split Pea Soup

P. Kevin Remington
August 2020

Once upon a time, not too long ago, there was a kingdom. Like all kingdoms, it had a castle way up high on a hill, and down below the castle was the village. Like all kingdoms, there was a royal family of a king, queen, prince, and Princess Stephanie. The royal family lived in the castle. The people of the kingdom lived in the village. It was a happy kingdom.

Everybody was very happy in this kingdom. In this kingdom, the people had a special food. It was the speciality of the whole kingdom. Everyone knew how to make this food. Everyone made it just a wee bit different so they could say theirs was the best. The specialty of the kingdom was split pea soup.

The king loved split pea soup.
The queen loved split pea soup.
The prince loved split pea soup.
Princess Stephanie, not so much.

Let me tell you about Princess Stephanie. Princess Stephanie is a very lovely young girl. She has a very nice smile and beautiful long black hair that hung down her back. She liked to play with children in the village, and they would jump rope, skip rocks in the stream, climb trees, fishing, and even wrestle. In fact, Princess Stephanie liked all the people in the village, and all the people in the village liked Princess Stephanie. The only two things that Princess Stephanie did not like were wearing princess clothes and split pea soup!

I should explain that princess clothes tend to get in the way. If you are trying to climb a tree and you cannot lift your leg because it is tangled in a big fluffy princess dress, that makes it much more difficult. Have you ever tried to skip rope in a big fluffy princess dress? You have to tuck the dress up under your arms or you will trip over it. If you tried to step into the stream while fishing, her big, fluffy princess dress would get soaked and go flump! That makes it very difficult to fish.

No, Princess Stephanie did not like wearing princess clothes. The only time the fluffy princess dress was good was when she was wrestling with the boys. They could not get around the dress, and she pinned them easily. Still, Princess Stephanie was very happy running and playing with the children.

Did I remember to tell you that in this kingdom, they made magnificent split pea soup? It was the best, anywhere, split pea soup. It was even the national food of the kingdom. Everybody in the kingdom loved the split pea soup.

All the villagers loved the soup.

The king loved the split pea soup.

The queen loved the split pea soup.

The prince loved the split pea soup.

Princess Stephanie, not so much.

Being as this was the food of the kingdom, everyone expected that everybody would love split pea soup. Everyone knew the royal family all loved split pea soup except Princess Stephanie, but everyone loved Princess Stephanie anyways.

One day, a cobbler and his family moved to the village. They had just moved to the village from over the hill. The cobbler, everyone soon found out, made wonderful shoes and boots.

Princess Stephanie was in need of new shoes and had heard about the cobbler who made wonderful shoes. Princess Stephanie went to the cobbler's house and knocked on the door.

"Knock! Knock! Knock!"

When the cobbler opened the door, Princess Stephanie said, "I need some new shoes, can you make a pair for me?"
The cobbler said "Come right in," and he measured her foot,
drew pictures, and said that the new shoes would be ready Tuesday.

While Princess Stephanie was getting measured, she notice the cobbler's son. He was a very handsome boy. Princess Stephanie had never seen him before about the village and thought she should make friends with him. So she did.

They went for a walk to the hills.

They went fishing in the stream.

They picked elderberries and strawberries and just had a wonderful afternoon.

That evening, as Princess Stephanie was about to head home to the castle, the cobbler's wife invited her to stay for dinner. The cobbler's wife had heard that split pea soup was the dish of the kingdom, and everyone loves split pea soup. The cobbler's wife asked a neighbour how to make split pea soup. She learned about boiling the water just right and adding the ingredients and stirring and simmering and making great split pea soup.

The cobbler and his family were not from the village. They had just moved to the village, and nobody had told them that Princess Stephanie does not like split pea soup.

When everyone sat down for dinner, they all got a big bowl of split pea soup, including Princess Stephanie because she was their special guest.

When Princess Stephanie saw the split pea soup in front of her, do you know what she did? She ate the split pea soup. In fact, she finished her whole bowl of split pea soup.

Princess Stephanie then told the cobbler's wife, "This is the finest split pea soup that I have had in a very long time."

Princess Stephanie did not lie. Princess Stephanie just had not eaten split pea soup in years because she does not like split pea soup.

When the cobbler's wife offered more soup to Princess Stephanie, she said "No, thank you. I have had enough" because she was a real princess and did not want to insult the cobbler's wife by telling her that she did not like split pea soup.

The next day, Princess Stephanie and the handsome boy went out to play again. They played ball with the other children. They ran about playing chase the frog. They just had a fun filled day.

At dinnertime, the cobbler's wife invited Princess Stephanie for dinner again.

Princess Stephanie said hesitantly, "Okay, thank you."

Once again, when everyone was seated, the cobbler's wife set out bowls of split pea soup for everyone. Once again, Princess Stephanie ate her whole bowl of split pea soup.

When the cobbler's wife offered Princess Stephanie some more soup, Princess Stephanie said, "No, thank you, I am quite full." Princess Stephanie was taught to be polite and eat what was put in front of her even if she did not like it.

The next day, while Princess Stephanie and the handsome boy were out playing, she told him that she really does not like split pea soup.

"What!" shouted the boy. "Split pea soup is the national food of the kingdom, and everybody loves split pea soup," sputtered the boy.

"I know," said Princess Stephanie. "My father, the king, and my mother, the queen, and even my brother, the prince, love split pea soup, but I do not," explained Princess Stephanie.

"Oh dear, and that is what my mom has been feeding you," sighed the boy.

Princess Stephanie tried to calm the boy and said, "That is okay, I will eat your mom's split pea soup."

The next day, when the cobbler's wife invited Princess Stephanie to dinner, Princess Stephanie was very concerned. She did not like split pea soup. She did not want to be rude and not go to dinner. Princess Stephanie thought and thought and in the end decided to accept the dinner invitation.

When everyone was seated, the food was set before each person. In front of the cobbler was placed a bowl of split pea soup. In front of the boy was placed a bowl of split pea soup. In front of Princess Stephanie was placed a peanut-butter-and-jam sandwich.

Princess Stephanie ate her peanut-butter-and-jam sandwich and had a big smile on her face as she said, "Thank you."

From that day forward, everyone in the kingdom knew Princess Stephanie did not like split pea soup.

The End

Gladys the Moose

P. Kevin Remington
July 2020

Once upon a time, Kyle and his family and his dog went up to Algonquin Park to go camping.

Every year, Kyle and his family and his dog would go to Algonquin Park to go camping. They would drive up to the lake and unload the car of camping gear and canoes. Then they would load all the camping gear into the canoes. Then they would set off across the lake.

They would paddle and paddle. Then they would paddle and paddle some more. It was a very large lake, and they would paddle past all the campers with cabins and motorboats. When they got to the other side of the lake, they would unload all their gear and portage across the trail to another lake.

They would put all their gear back in their canoes and start paddling again across this lake. They would paddle and paddle until they were even past the people who camp with lawn chairs. When they got to the other side of the lake, they would unload all their gear and portage across the trail to another lake.

They would put all their gear back in their canoes and start paddling again and paddle and paddle until they found just the right campsite. This year, they found the perfect campsite on a little lake called Otter Slide. In this lake, there was a small island. On this island was the perfect place to camp.

There they unloaded all their camping gear and set up camp. They put up their two tents. They hung a hammock. They set up a campfire. They hung their food high in a tree so animals could not get to it. When everything was all set up just the way they liked it, they went swimming.

The next day, the family decided to go paddling around the lake for day trip and see what they find out in the wilderness. Everyone got into the canoes for the day trip, except for Kyle.

Kyle was very tired and said, "I am very tired. I paddled harder than anybody yesterday. I am going to lay in this hammock and have a nap."

And he did.

The rest of the family went on their day trip.

On the same lake, Otter Slide, lived a moose named Gladys. Gladys liked Otter Slide because she could swim in the water. She would eat the tasty tree leaves and bark around the lake. Gladys really enjoyed going for a walk through the shallow water beside her favourite island then up across the island.

On this day, when Gladys went for her walk, she crossed through the shallow water to her favourite island, and as she was walking across the island, she saw two tents. She did not know why there were tents on her favourite island, so she put her nose in the tents to see what was in them. That was all she could fit in the tents because they were much too small for a moose. Then she walked a little further and saw food hanging way up in a tree. Gladys thought that was very strange. Then she walked through the campsite and saw shoes and books and a campfire all set up. Then Gladys noticed the hammock.

Gladys had never seen a hammock before. She sniffed the hammock. She noticed that it went from one tree to another tree. In the middle, it looked kind of lumpy, so she sniffed it and bumped it with her nose. It was then that she noticed inside the hammock was a human.

There was Kyle sleeping. Gladys did not know what a Kyle sleeping was. She snuffled a bit at the feet. She snuffled at his belly button. She snuffled his face. Then Gladys wanted to know if a Kyle would be tasty, so she licked him all the way from his chin to his forehead.

Then Kyle woke up, with a start, and said, "Yikes! A moose!" Then he fainted.

That startled Gladys, and she said, "Yikes!"

Gladys then jumped up, ran around the campsite, twice around the tents, jumped in the water, and swam to the other side of the lake.

When the family and the family dog returned from their day trip, Kyle was all excited and told them that a moose came to their campsite. And a moose licked his face. And…

"Yah, ya, ya," said the family, not believing Kyle.

The family had seen a moose on their trip. They had seen a great big bull moose with a full rack of antlers. It was down the creek and was a very magnificent animal, so they were sure that there would be no moose in their campsite.

Kyle tried to convince them, but nobody would believe him

The next day, everyone relaxed at the campsite. They went swimming. They ate s'mores. They just had a very quiet, relaxing day.

The day after that, Gladys walked through the water. She walked up on to her favourite island. She saw the campsite and walked all the way around the campsite. Gladys saw Kyle. She smiled at Kyle. Kyle waved to Gladys. Then Gladys jumped in the water and swam to the other side of the lake and was gone.

Everybody at the campsite were frozen. They were in shock with their eyes wide open and their mouths wide open, and they all looked at Kyle. Then they all looked at where the moose was swimming away.

Then they all turned to Kyle and said, "We are so sorry that we did not believe you. That was a moose!"

Kyle just smiled and said "Yup!" then went and had a nap in the hammock.

The End

Cheri y la
Hamburguesa con Queso

P. Kevin Remington
July 2020

When Cheri was little girl, she loved to go biking. She would ride her bike all the way down to the corner because she was five and was allowed to go to the corner. She would then bike all the way back to the other corner because she was very good at biking.

When Cheri went biking, she would see all sorts of things Cheri would see her house and the flowers in front of the house and the little garden gnomes standing in the gardens at front of the house. She saw her neighbour's house, and it had a trellis with lots of flowers growing all over it. When she made it to the corner, she would see the temple building right there on the corner. That is where they went to meet every Saturday.

Cheri was very proud that she could bike all the way from corner to corner.

One day, Cheri and her family went out for dinner. They went to McDonald's. That was Cheri's favourite restaurant because they had marvelous food and toys for children.

They had fries, which were really good.

They had apple pies, which were really good.

They had Big Macs, which were really, really good.

There was also a bacon cheeseburger that looked really good. Cheri had never had the bacon cheeseburger. Cheri wanted to try a bacon cheeseburger because she had heard that they were really the best.

Cheri asked her dad, "Dad, can I have bacon cheeseburger today? I hear they are really good."

Cheri's Dad said, "No, you cannot have any bacon. We do not eat bacon."

Cheri was confused and asked, "Why?"

Her dad answered, "Because we are Jewish, and Jews do not eat bacon. So I am sorry, but you cannot have a bacon cheeseburger."

Cheri was still confused and asked again, "Why?"

Her dad explained that there were laws that Jews follow, and one of the laws was not to eat bacon. Cheri was very sad. Cheri kept asking why, and she kept getting answers that she did not understand. After all, Cheri was only five years old.

Cheri had a Big Mac instead, and it was really good, but she really wanted that bacon cheeseburger.

When the family got home, Cheri got on her bicycle and thought that maybe there might be a better answer at the temple.

Cheri biked all the way to the temple on the corner. Then she went up to the door and knocked.

Blam! Blam! Blam!

When the rabbi answered the door, Cheri said, "Rabbi, I have a question."

The rabbi said, "Yes, what is your question?"

Cheri said, "My dad will not let me eat a bacon cheeseburger. I wanted a bacon cheeseburger because I hear that they are really tasty. Why can I not have a bacon cheeseburger?"

The rabbi explained, "They might be tasty. I have not had one myself. I am Jewish. You are Jewish. Jewish people do not eat meat from a pig. Bacon comes from a pig, so we do not eat it."

Cheri whined, "But it is very tasty. My friends say it is very tasty. Why do we not eat bacon?"

The rabbi proceeded to tell Cheri a story. He said, "You remember Moses? We talked about Moses and how he parted the waters of the Red Sea and led the Israelites across the desert. Before Moses did that, he lived in Egypt, and he tried to follow the laws of Egypt. However, Moses did not like what the Egyptian laws were doing to the Israelites. So Moses ran away. Much like you ran away from your house all the way down here to the temple. Moses ran much further. He ran all the way into the wilderness. In the wilderness, Moses thought now he could do whatever he wanted. But G-d had a different plan for Moses. G-d put a bush in front of Moses. The bush looked like it was on fire because there were flames, but the bush did not seem to burn. Moses did not know what to do.

"G-d knew what to do. G-d said, 'Moses, take your shoes off because you are standing in a very special place.' And Moses did what G-d asked. And Moses and G-d had a chat right there. G-d told Moses, 'If you follow my rules and laws, I will take care of you.' We all know what happened after that. Moses followed the rules and laws and went and got the Israelites out of Egypt. We all know that story. Cheri, you know that story."

Cheri nodded her head.

The rabbi continued, "That is like your bacon cheeseburger. Moses did not understand why G-d wanted him to do the things he did, but he did them to follow the rules and laws. You may not understand why your dad will not let you eat a bacon cheeseburger but know that he is looking after you."

After that talk with the rabbi, Cheri got on her bicycle and biked all the way home. She went into the house and saw her dad sitting on his chair.

Cheri said, "Daddy, I still want a bacon cheeseburger, but I love you."

"I love you too," said her dad.

Cheri never did have a bacon cheeseburger.

The End

The Babysitter

P. Kevin Remington
July 2020

K evin was a nice old man who lived in the neighbourhood.
In the wintertime, Kevin would carefully shovel his sidewalk so people could safely walk without slipping. In the summertime, he would sit on his front porch and drink hot Earl Grey tea and watch the sunsets. When people walked by, Kevin would always smile and wave to them and say, "Hi." In the fall, he would pick his elderberries and make elderberry pies and share it with his neighbours.

Kevin was just a nice, quiet old man who lived in the neighbourhood.

One day, his neighbour, Susan, asked if he could watch her daughter, Addison, for a little while. Susan had a doctor's appointment, and she could not take her daughter with her.

Kevin thought about this for a moment and said that he could do this, watch Addison. After all, Kevin had babysat his grandson, Turner. When Turner came over, they sat together and had a nice cup of tea, played chess, watched a movie, and had a lovely time. Kevin and Turner had more tea and chatted until it was time for Turner to go home with his parents. Kevin remembered this fondly and thought that it would be good to babysit Addison.

The next day, when Addison was to come over to his house, Kevin was ready. He had made tea. He had the chess set all up ready to be played. He was ready to take care of Addison.

When Addison arrived, Kevin asked, "What would you like to do today?"

Addison quickly answered, "I want to play a game."

"What game would you like to play?" asked Kevin.

"Hide-and-go-seek," answered Addison. She went on to explain how to play, "You count to thirty, and I will go hide."

Kevin covered his eyes, and he counted to thirty then went to look for Addison.

Addison was just a little girl, only about six or seven years old. She was not a very good hider. In fact, she hid behind the curtains in the living room and Kevin, could see her shoes sticking out under the curtains.

Kevin did not want to find Addison right away because he thought that would not make the game very fun. Kevin looked everywhere and announced where he was looking so Addison could hear him.

Kevin looked on the couch and said, "Nope, no Addison on the couch."

Next, Kevin looked in the tea cups and said loudly, "No Addison in the teacups."

At that point, Kevin heard a little giggle behind the curtains

Kevin went to the giggle and drew back the curtains and shouted, "I found you!"

Addison laughed with joy and explained, "Now you hide."

Kevin did not really want to hide and suggested that they do something else.

"Why do we not make cookies?" suggested Kevin.

Addison was so excited and said, "Yes, I love making chocolate chip cookies."

Kevin got out a little stool for Addison to stand on so she could reach the counter. Then they started to make cookies. Kevin got out a big bowl. They had to put the flour in the bowl. Kevin let Addison help with measuring the flour into bowl.

Addison was having great fun, and soon the flour was in the bowl, on the counter, in the sink, over the cupboards, and generally everywhere.

Next, it was time to break the eggs and put them in the bowl. The recipe only called for two eggs, but Addison sort of dropped one egg. Another egg rolled off the end of the counter and smashed on the floor. And somehow an egg wound up in the light fixture on the ceiling. Two eggs did make it into the bowl.

Next, they added the milk. This time, Kevin added that carefully.

Then it was time to add the sugar, cocoa powder, and finally chocolate chips. The right amount of sugar and cocoa powder might have gotten in the bowl. There were definitely signs of sugar and cocoa powder all over the counter and floor. They only needed one cup of chocolate chips.

Addison had to test the chocolate chips to make sure they were tasty enough. Then she had to test the chocolate chips to make sure they were the right hardness. And it was only Kevin who managed to save enough chocolate chips for the cookies. Addison had a mouthful of chocolate chips and could not say anything.

After everything was in the bowl and mixed up really well, Addison helped to plop them on a pan to be baked in the oven. There were large plops. There were small plops. There were plops that flew through the air and stuck to the refrigerator.

Finally, Kevin had Addison stand back because the oven was very hot, and he put the plops of cookies in to be baked.

When the chocolate chip cookies were ready to come out, Kevin suggested that perhaps they should eat a couple, just to make sure they were tasty enough.

Addison said, "Yes! I would like some milk to dip my cookies. My daddy always dips his cookies."

Kevin got two glasses of milk. One for him and one for Addison, and they dipped cookies and ate chocolate chip cookies.

After the milk and cookies, Kevin thought they could read a book or watch a movie and just relax.

Kevin asked Addison, "What would you like to do now?"

Addison said, "I want to play a game. I want to play hide-and-go-seek."

Kevin counted to thirty again, and Addison went off hiding.

Kevin checked behind the curtains, and there was no Addison. He checked on top of the couch, and there was no Addison. He checked under the couch, and there was no Addison. Then Kevin noticed all these little white foot prints from all the spilt flour from making cookies.

Kevin followed the foot prints all over the house. The footprints went in the bathroom then out to the garage. The footprints went from the garage to the basement. The footprints went from the basement to bedroom. The footprints finally stopped in the family room.

Kevin found Addison under the rug in the family room.

Kevin then said, "Why do we not play a game I like? Would you like to play chess?"

Addison had a queer look on her face and said, "Chess? How do you play chess?"

Kevin explained that you sit at this table with the chessboard and you move the pieces.

Addison said that she loved moving pieces. Then she picked up the horse and asked what it does in the game.

Kevin explained that was a knight, and it moved forward and sideways. Addison grabbed both of her knights and had them hopping all over the board. Then Addison lifted another piece.

"What is this?" asked Addison.

"That is a pawn, and it can only move forward," explained Kevin.

Suddenly, Addison moved all her pawns forward. Then Addison asked about another piece.

"That is a rook," said Kevin, "and he goes straight or sideways."

Addison took her rook and blasted through all the pawns. Her rook blasted through all the knights. In fact, her rook blasted through everything and knocked it all onto the rug. This was not exactly the peaceful game of chess that Kevin had expected.

"Since we finished this game, what would you like to do now?" asked Kevin.

Addison did not hesitate and said, "I want to play hide-and-go-seek!"

Kevin took a deep breath. He sighed a huge sigh. Then Kevin counted to thirty, and Addison went off to hide.

This time, Kevin looked everywhere for Addison. He looked behind the curtains. He looked on the couch. He looked under the cushions on the couch. He looked behind the door in the bathroom. He looked under the rug.

Kevin looked everywhere and could not find Addison anywhere. He was starting to get concerned, but just before Susan returned, Kevin heard a giggle. Kevin slowly looked up to where the giggle was, and there was Addison on the chandelier. Kevin has no idea how Addison got up there, but he managed to get her down safely.

Just as Kevin and Addison were going to sit down and have more milk and cookies, Susan came and opened the door. Susan saw some white flour on the walls over here. And she noticed white flour on the couch. And she noticed a cloud of white flour gently coming down the stairs. Then Susan noticed Kevin and Addison.

There Addison sat in her best summery dress with pretty flowers, all covered in white powder looking more like a ghost than a little girl.

Susan carefully asked, "Was Addison any trouble?"

Kevin answered with a smile, "Oh no. Addison was no trouble at all. We made cookies and played games, and we had a lovely time."

Susan shook her head slowly while looking at all the white flour everywhere and took Addison home.

Kevin set about cleaning his house. It took him all week to clean up all the flour and milk and sugar and cocoa powder that was all through the house. Finally, when the house was almost all back to normal, Kevin found that he lost the two rooks from his chess set. He is not sure where they are.

I think one is on the chandelier.

The End

Stephanie Gets Santa

P. Kevin Remington
July 2020

This is the year that Stephanie was going to meet Santa Clause. Stephanie has seen the Santas at the mall, but everybody knows that the Santas at the mall are not the real Santa; they are just helpers for the real Santa Claus.

This year, Stephanie was going to meet the real Santa. She was going to capture him when he comes to her house. Stephanie is not allowed to stay up real late. Her bedtime is eight o'clock, and Santa usually comes much later at night. Stephanie did not want to miss him this year, so she had a plan.

Stephanie waited until it was almost bedtime. Then she set her plan into action. Stephanie had planned traps to capture Santa.

Stephanie put her Barbie dolls by the front door in case Santa came in through the front door. She placed her dolls, car, and play-house right inside the door. If Santa came in that way, he would trip on the toys and fall and make lots of noise.

Santa was tricky, Stephanie knew. Just in case Santa came in through the front window, she put Lego bricks on the window sill and on the floor just below the window. She used all her Lego bricks and some of her brother's dinosaur Lego bricks and spread them out carefully.

This was a good plan, but Stephanie knew that her parents are tricky too. Stephanie was sure her parents would help out Santa, so she made a trap for her parents. Stephanie put all her marbles on the stairs to her parents' bedroom. She put all her aggies on one step. Her steelies on another. She put the pretty star eyes on another step and the cat eyes on the bottom step. And just to make sure, Stephanie put tiny tacks around the edges.

Stephanie wanted to make sure that if it was Santa, or her parents, that they were going to make a lot of noise and wake her up.

The last part of Stephanie's plan was to move the couch out from the wall. Behind the couch, Stephanie had a blanket and pillow. That was where Stephanie and her dog, Josie, were going to sleep that night. When Santa came and made a lot of noise, it would wake up Josie, and Josie would wake up Stephanie, and she would meet the real Santa Claus.

Stephanie thought this was a perfect plan.

That night, the night before Christmas, Stephanie put out the glass of milk for Santa. She put out a plate of cookies for Santa. She put out a carrot and carefully laid it beside the plate. The carrot was for the reindeer. Then Stephanie went to sleep behind the couch.

It did not seem like a very long time when Stephanie was awakened by a terrible loud racket. It was just like the book Stephanie's father had read to her. Out in the yard, there was a terrible noise. Stephanie jumped up to see what had made all the noise.

It was dark, and Stephanie could not see anything. She turned on the light, and there sprawled out on the floor was her father. Stephanie's father had gotten up to get a snack from the fridge and slipped on the marbles, tripped over the tacks, landed on the Lego bricks, and fell down. Flump! Right in front of the Christmas tree. He had landed so hard that he even knocked over the cookies and milk that were for Santa.

The plan was ruined, and Stephanie was never going to meet Santa. So Stephanie went upstairs to her bedroom and fell asleep. She slept very peacefully knowing that she had a new plan for next year.

In the morning, Stephanie ran downstairs to see if Santa Claus had come. Santa had come, and there were presents under the tree and her father fast asleep behind the couch.

The End

About the Author

Kevin Remington is a father of two children. Though they are much older now, when they were very young, he did not find stories and books that he liked for children. He told his own stories.

Throughout the years, he has told many stories. Many of the stories were told around a campfire in Algonquin Park on their family camping trips.

He has been a computer nerd for most of his adult life. As such, one of the requirements was to have a hobby that had nothing to do with computers. His were books, comics, graphic novels, and writing. He could add music and golfing to the list, though he does not do those well at all.

To know him, you just sit with him with a cup of Earl Grey tea, and you will talk and tell tales, to delight, and put a smile on your face.